There were **buttons** to **push.**
There were **levers** to **pull.**
There were boots and a helmet
to wear, too!

Only three children could play at a time.
But **everyone** wanted a turn!

Then Miss Clover had a good idea.
She put everyone's name in a hat.

She pulled out Nora's name first.

She pulled out Dan's name second.

She pulled out Henry's name third.

Miss Clover said they could play first.
But they had to **take turns** and **share.**

Nora put on the boots and the helmet.

She pushed all the
buttons.

She pulled all the
levers.

She wouldn't let Dan or Henry take turns.

She wouldn't let them wear the **boots** or the **helmet.**

Dan got **mad.**
He said it wasn't fair.
He pushed **Nora hard!**

Henry got **mad.**
He said it wasn't fair.
He grabbed **the helmet!**

Nora got very, **very mad!**
She said it wasn't fair.
She said she **didn't** want to share!

Miss Clover got **mad.**
She sent them out.

Nora went to the Reading Corner.
Soon she stopped feeling mad.
She wished that she had taken turns
playing with Henry and Dan.

Dan went to the Art Corner.
Soon he stopped feeling mad.
He wished that he had not
pushed Nora.

Henry went on the computer. Soon he stopped feeling mad. He wished that he had not grabbed the helmet.

Miss Clover counted slowly to ten.
Soon she stopped feeling mad, too!

Nora, Dan, and Henry said "I'm sorry"
to Miss Clover and to each other.

Miss Clover let them have another turn
in the Space Station.

She told them to **take turns** and **share.**

They all took turns pushing the **buttons.**

They all took turns pulling the **levers.**

They all shared the **helmet** and the **boots.**

They had lots of **fun.**

And this time, no one got mad at **all!**

Can you tell the story of what happens when these two space creatures find a toy they don't want to share?

How do you think they felt when they didn't share the toy? How did they feel at the end?

A note about sharing this book

The **Our Emotions and Behavior** series has been developed to provide a starting point for further discussion about children's feelings and behavior, in relation both to themselves and to other people.

Not Fair, Won't Share
This story explores sharing in a reassuring way. It examines the problems that can come up when people don't share—especially the angry response that being selfish can generate. It also looks at how people can stop feeling angry.

The book aims to encourage children to work as a group or class, taking turns and sharing fairly. It promotes awareness of behavioral expectations in this setting and of the consequences of children's words and actions for themselves and others. The book also explores how to express and control feelings in appropriate ways.

Picture story
The picture story on pages 22 and 23 provides an opportunity for speaking and listening. Children are encouraged to tell the story illustrated in the panels: when two little space creatures find a toy, they each want it. One grabs it away, and then the other grabs it back. But it is not until they share the toy that playing with it becomes fun.

How to use the book
The book is designed for adults to share with either an individual child or a group of children, and as a starting point for discussion.

The book also provides visual support and repeated words and phrases to build confidence in children who are starting to read on their own.

Before reading the story
Choose a time to read when you and the children are relaxed and have time to share the story.

Spend time looking at the illustrations and talking about what the book may be about before reading it together.

After reading, talk about the book with the children

- What was it about? Have the children ever been selfish when playing with others? Why do they think it is important to share and to let others take turns?

- Extend this discussion by talking about other things that children find hard to share. Do they find it hard to share toys with friends or with siblings? What things do they like and dislike about sharing with others? Remind them it may not only be material things that they find hard to share. They may, for example, find it hard to share a parent's attention with a sibling.

- Talk about the steps each character took to stop feeling angry. Point out that adults, too, feel angry and have to find ways of controlling their feelings.

- Talk about the things that make children feel angry. Spend time discussing ways of controlling anger. Some may find it best to leave the room, count to ten, or distract themselves with another activity. Encourage the children to share their experiences and their tried and tested solutions for anger management.

- Talk with children about the importance of saying "I'm sorry" to a person who is upset by their actions, and how this can make the person feel better.

- Look at the picture story. Talk about how each little space creature felt when the other would not share the toy.

- Talk about other things that are better to share than to have or play with on their own.

- Play a game that involves sharing and taking turns, such as a simple card or board game. Or sing a round such as "Are You Sleeping?" or "Row, Row, Row Your Boat."

Library of Congress Cataloging-in-Publication Data
Graves, Sue, 1950–
    Not fair, won't share / written by Sue Graves ; illustrated by Desideria Guicciardini.
        p. cm. — (Our emotions and behavior)
    ISBN 978-1-57542-375-3
    1. Sharing in children—Juvenile literature. I. Guicciardini, Desideria, ill. II. Title.
    BF723.S428G73 2011
    152.4—dc22   2011001566

Reading Level Grades 1–2; Interest Level Ages 4–8; Fountas & Pinnell Guided Reading Level I

10 9 8 7 6 5 4 3 2 1
Printed in China
S14100311

Free Spirit Publishing Inc.
217 Fifth Avenue North, Suite 200
Minneapolis, MN 55401-1299
(612) 338-2068
help4kids@freespirit.com
www.freespirit.com

First published in 2011 by Franklin Watts, a division of Hachette Children's Books · London, UK, and Sydney, Australia

Text © Franklin Watts 2011
Illustrations © Desideria Guicciardini 2011

The rights of Sue Graves to be identified as the author and Desideria Guicciardini as the illustrator of this Work have
been asserted in accordance with the Copyright, Designs and Patents Act, 1988.

Editors: Adrian Cole and Jackie Hamley
Designers: Peter Scoulding and Jonathan Hair